By Leslie Zimmerman

Illustrated by Paige Briscoe

BLUE HOUSE PUBLISHING 11 N 500 W.
Springville, UT 84663

For information regarding bulk purchases, send a request to Blue House Publishing, or email us at BCCrow@BlueHPublishing.com

Library of Congress Control Number: 2016945101

ISBN-13   978-1-943239-06-1
ISBN-10   1-943239-06-1

For Jameson and Amaryllis
Big or small, have courage to follow your dreams. -PB

For my kids, never stop dreaming. -LZ

I think someday I'll be a G.I.
I'll wear camouflage and crawl through the sand,
maybe I'll go to a faraway land.

I'll conquer the enemy like
great grandpa Charley,
who dad, once said
was in the Army.

I might like to be a
high fashion designer
Some clothes are fine,
but mine would be finer.

I'll sew other's clothes
from their heads to their toes,
I'll add on some zippers and buttons and bows.
The possibilities are endless,
because I am fearless.

I bet bee keepers have a great time,
buzzing with bees while they make sweet honey.
After all, there's nothing I like as much as honey.
So sticky, so runny and oh so yummy!

I could be a veterinarian in a white coat;

I'll save the lives of turtles, kittens, puppies and goats.

Someday I might be a great business owner;
I'll set my own hours, a go-it-a-loner.
Maybe I could start a business that cheers people up;
The way that Mom does when I'm feeling amuck.

Or perhaps I will have a job in the sky,
a pilot who flies from LA to Shanghai.

Maybe I'll be a protector;
A fireman, EMT, or safety inspector.

 I could cure some diseases and make people better,
a true saint, a healer,
a give people a meal-er.

Give me some brushes and I'll be an artist.
I'd paint your portrait with a flick of my wrist.

I'll be a baker and make you a pie.
Or maybe a cake 10 stories high.

Brriiing! the bell rang, it was time to go.
I grabbed my bag and headed home.
The few blocks to home, I walked alone,
thinking of things I could be when grown.
When I got to my house,
my mom greeted me.

We talked of the choices I might like to be;
an astronaut, a bee keeper, baker, EMT.

With a big grin she said this to me;
  "Whatever it is you choose to be,
for you my love will always be free."

So,
I think just for now
I'll stick to being a kid.
After all, this is a pretty sweet gig.

There is plenty of time to live and to learn
of the things I could do when I am big.

Besides, without me, who would make my mom smile?
That is the best job, by far, for miles and miles.

CPSIA information can be obtained
at www.ICGtesting.com
Printed in the USA
LVOW06*2302081116
512207LV00012B/33/P